The Once-Upon-a-Time Dragon

by the same author
THE SCRIBBLE MONSTER

The Once-Upon-a-Time Dragon

JACK KENT

BEDTIME STORIES

HARCOURT BRACE JOVANOVICH, PUBLISHERS   ●   SAN DIEGO   NEW YORK   LONDON

For JACK 2,
the artist in
the family.

Requests for permission to make copies of
any part of the work should be mailed to:
Permissions, Harcourt Brace Jovanovich, Publishers,
Orlando, Florida 32887

Printed in the United States of America

LIBRARY OF CONGRESS CATALOGING
IN PUBLICATION DATA

Kent, Jack, 1920–
The once-upon-a-time dragon.
Summary: Convinced he is under a magic spell, a
dragon buys a body-building guide in order to
transform himself into a man.
[1. Dragons—Fiction.   2. Bodybuilding—Fiction]
I. Title.
PZ7.K4140n   [E]   82-2983
ISBN 0-15-332875-4   (Library: 10 different titles)
ISBN 0-15-332893-2   (Single title, 4 copies)
ISBN 0-15-332953-X   (Replacement single copy)

There was once a dragon named Sam, who was very fond of bedtime stories. He liked them so much that he went to bed 87 times a day, so it was almost always time for another story.

The stories he liked best were of course the ones with dragons in them. Sam noticed that the dragons often turned out to be handsome princes under a magic spell.

Sam wondered whether *he* might be
a handsome prince under a magic spell,
but he thought it unlikely. There
aren't many handsome princes
in the world these days.
But he wondered whether
he might be a reasonably
good-looking president or
even a famous rock star.

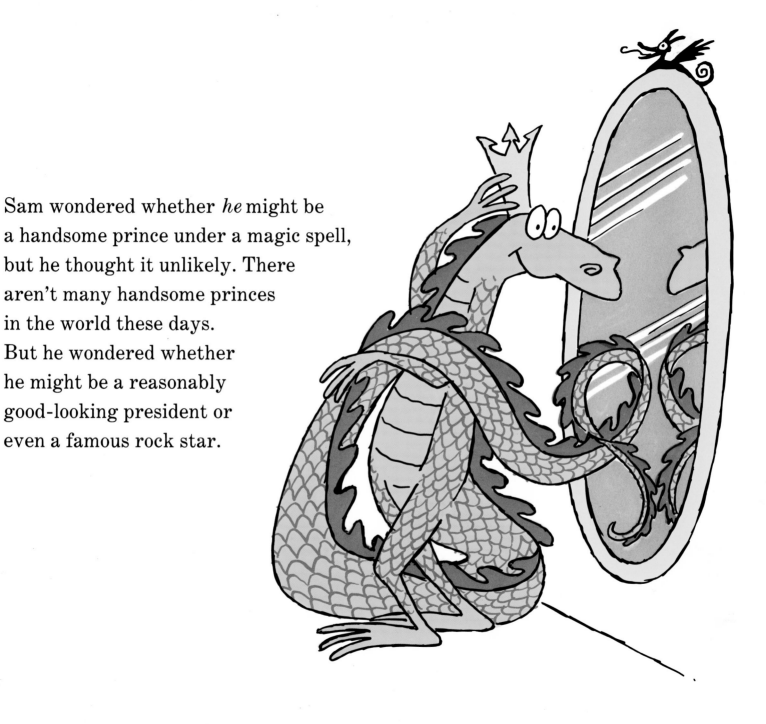

Whenever he thought about the possibility of becoming a man, Sam got so excited that he breathed fire.

And the more he thought about it, the surer
he became that he was under a magic spell.
But how was he to become a man?

He tried everything he could think of.
But no matter how hard he tried, he couldn't
break the spell.

Then one day he saw something exciting in a magazine.

It was an advertisement for a body-building course. It said, "Be the man you want to become." And it guaranteed results in only 30 days.

Sam subscribed to the course, and while he was waiting for it to come in the mail, he tried to decide what man he wanted to become.

The happiest man Sam knew was Mr. Johnson, who sat on a park bench on warm afternoons and fed popcorn to the pigeons. "*That's* the man I want to become," said Sam.

So when the package arrived, he worked hard on the body-building course.

And, sure enough, in only 30 days
he became the man he wanted to become.

That was a bit annoying to Mr. Johnson, who rather logically argued that he had thought of it first.

However, he wasn't a selfish man and finally agreed to share. So Mr. Johnson fed the pigeons on Mondays, Wednesdays, and Fridays, and every other Saturday. And Sam took his place on the other days. The pigeons couldn't tell the difference.

One day Sam forgot whose turn it was and went to the park on Mr. Johnson's day. He got so upset that he breathed fire, not having broken himself of the habit.

"That's very clever!" said Mr. Johnson.
"Have you ever thought of joining the circus?"

"Not yet," said Sam, "but I will."

And he thought of it on his
very next afternoon off
from feeding the pigeons.
Sam went to the circus manager's
office and breathed fire for him.

The manager was slightly singed and very impressed.

Sam got the job with the circus . . .

and soon became the star attraction.

Everybody came to see the man who breathed fire. Even Mr. Johnson came sometimes.

But Sam was so busy being famous that he
neglected his body-building exercises.
And one day, during the matinee performance . . .

he turned back into a dragon.

Sam lost his job
at the circus.
After all, there isn't any
novelty in a *dragon* breathing fire.

Mr. Johnson said he was sorry
Sam wasn't a man anymore.
But Sam didn't care.
"I'm much more comfortable
just being myself," he said.

On warm afternoons you will find Sam and
Mr. Johnson sitting together on a park bench.
They take turns feeding popcorn to the pigeons
and reading bedtime stories to each other.

And the stories they like best are the ones with dragons in them.